Magic
Animal Friends

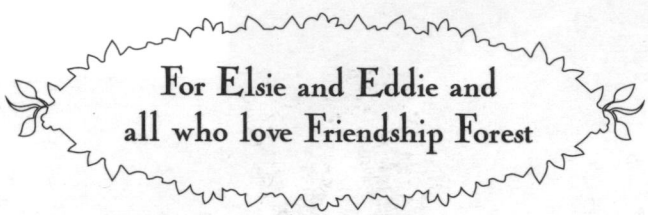

For Elsie and Eddie and
all who love Friendship Forest

Special thanks to Valerie Wilding

ORCHARD BOOKS

First published in Great Britain in 2018 by The Watts Publishing Group

1 3 5 7 9 10 8 6 4 2

Text copyright © Working Partners Ltd 2018
Illustrations copyright © Working Partners Ltd 2018
Series created by Working Partners Ltd

A CIP catalogue record for this book is available from the British Library.

ISBN 978 1 40834 716 4

Printed in Great Britain

MIX
Paper from
responsible sources
FSC® C104740

The paper and board used in this book are made from wood from responsible sources

Orchard Books
An imprint of Hachette Children's Group
Part of The Watts Publishing Group Limited
Carmelite House, 50 Victoria Embankment, London EC4Y 0DZ

An Hachette UK Company
www.hachette.co.uk
www.hachettechildrens.co.uk

Imogen Scribblewhiskers' Perfect Picture

Daisy Meadows

ORCHARD

N

Toadstool Glade

Bluebell
Brook

Friendship
Tree

Bobblehop Barn

Billy Stoutfoot's
Cobblers

Nibblesqueak Bakery

Boggit
Swamp

The Whizzpaws'
Tower

Grizelda's
Tower

Friendship Forest
Weather Station

Scribble Thicket

Stationery Station

Toadstool Cafe

Cleverfeather's ...nting Shed

WoollyhopShop

Forest Halt Station

HarmonyHall Theatre

...asure ...ree

Moo-Moo Milkshake Hut

Garland Green

Sparklepaw Cottage

Map of Friendship Forest

Can you keep a secret? I thought you could!

Then I'll tell you about an enchanted wood.

It lies through the door in the old oak tree,

Let's go there now - just follow me!

We'll find adventure that never ends,

And meet the Magic Animal Friends!

Love,
Goldie the Cat

Contents

CHAPTER ONE

A Special Invitation

It was a sunny spring day and Lily Hart was sitting outside Helping Paw Wildlife Hospital with her best friend, Jess Forester. Two fluffy fox cubs were playing tug-of-war with a red chewy bone. The cubs were orphans, and were being cared for at Helping Paw until they were old enough

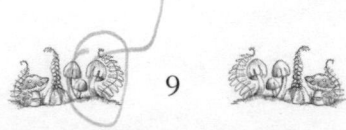

to return to the wild.

"They're so funny," Lily giggled, as one of the cubs dropped the bone and whirled around, chasing his bushy tail.

"Cute, too!" said Jess. "And they're growing fast."

Lily's parents ran the hospital from a barn at the bottom of their garden. They looked after all sorts of sick and injured animals. Jess and Lily loved helping to care for them.

The second fox cub batted the bone

10

into Lily's mum's vegetable garden, where it disappeared among the broccoli plants. Jess jumped up to fetch it, but a golden paw batted the bone back.

She gasped in delight. "Goldie!"

A beautiful green-eyed cat with glossy golden fur emerged from the rows of vegetables. Goldie had shown the girls the way to a secret world called Friendship Forest. It was a magical place where the animals lived in little cottages and dens, went to school, and drank blackberry fizz in the Toadstool Café. Best of all, the animals could talk!

When Goldie reached the girls, they kneeled to stroke her golden head. She leaned against them, purring.

"It's lovely to see you," Jess said.

Goldie mewed, then darted towards Brightley Stream at the bottom of the garden.

"Let's go!" cried Lily. "Goldie's taking us on another adventure in Friendship Forest!"

The girls ran after their friend. No time passed when they were in Friendship Forest, so they knew their parents wouldn't be worried. Goldie skipped over the

 12

stepping stones that crossed the stream, Lily and Jess skipping after her, into Brightley Meadow.

Goldie headed for the dead-looking oak tree in the centre. As she reached it, it burst into life. Bright green leaves and pale pink blossom sprang from every twig. A family of bluetits twittered in the branches, and in the grass, a butterfly alighted on a tiny froglet's head, then joined the plump bees buzzing among the branches.

The Friendship Tree!

As the girls caught up, Goldie touched

 13

the tree with her paw. Two words appeared in the bark and Jess and Lily read them aloud. "Friendship Forest!"

Immediately, a door appeared in the trunk. Jess reached for its leaf-shaped handle and opened it. Shimmering golden light shone out and Goldie leaped inside.

The girls clasped hands and followed. They felt a familiar tingle, and knew they were becoming a little smaller.

The golden light faded. Jess and Lily were in a sun-warmed forest clearing, surrounded by bushes dancing with blossoms. Tall pink flowers filled the air

with the scent of candyfloss. Animals

were bustling through the clearing –

a family of frogs, wearing different

coloured swimsuits, croaked, "Hello!"

as they hopped past. Jess waved to Mrs

Twinkletail the mouse, who hurried by clutching a basket filled with redcurrants.

"Welcome back!" she squeaked to the girls.

"Yes," said a soft, gentle voice behind them. "Welcome back."

"Goldie!" the girls said together.

Their cat friend had transformed so that she stood on her hind paws, almost reaching the girls' shoulders. A glittery scarf was draped around her neck, setting off her sparkling green eyes.

"It's lovely to be here!" cried Jess, as the girls hugged Goldie.

Lily clasped her hands together anxiously.

"Is Grizelda causing trouble again?" she asked.

Grizelda was a bad witch. She wanted to get rid of all the animals so she could have Friendship Forest for herself, and make it horrible and witchy. So far, Jess and Lily had managed to stop her, but Grizelda was always thinking up new, wicked plans.

Goldie shook her head. "I don't think

so," she said. "No one's seen her in the forest for a while."

"Good!" said Jess. "Let's hope she stays in her nasty tower."

"I haven't brought you here because of Grizelda," explained Goldie. "It's for something lovely." She turned, calling, "Imogen!"

From behind the candyfloss bush leaped an adorable black and white kitten with sparkling blue eyes and a beautiful floral garland hanging over one fluffy ear.

"Hi!" she said, waving a paw. "I'm Imogen Scribblewhiskers!"

 18

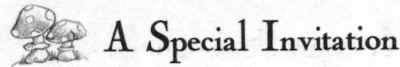

Jess smiled. "Hello, Imogen."

"I love your pretty garland," said Lily.

"Thanks," said the kitten with a

grin. "Goldie gave it to me. She's my godmother! And today's my birthday!"

"Happy birthday!" the girls said.

The kitten bounced in delight, her whiskers quivering. "I'm having a party. Would you like to come? Please say yes!"

Jess and Lily looked at each other, eyes shining. "Yes, please! We'd love to!"

CHAPTER TWO

Unwelcome Guests

Imogen dipped her paw into the silver bag she was carrying, and took out a scroll of violet paper.

"Here's your invitation, Jess," she said, handing it to her. "I made it myself." She fished in the pouch again, then looked around with a puzzled frown. "I must

 21

have dropped your invitation, Lily," she said. "But you're coming, aren't you?"

"Of course!" Lily hugged her.

Imogen purred happily.

"We can share my invitation," said Jess. She unrolled it and read:

Dear Jess,

Please come to my party at four o'clock this afternoon at the Toadstool Café.

Love,

Imogen

It was decorated with pictures of balloons and birthday cakes that Imogen had cut out from other pictures and

paintings and stuck on to the paper.

"What a lovely collage!" Lily said, peering over Jess's shoulder. "You're so talented."

"Thanks!" said Imogen. "My whole family love art. Mum and Dad are both great at drawing."

The girls, Goldie and Imogen set off along a path edged with starflowers and pink daffodils, heading towards Toadstool Glade and the party. As they walked,

Goldie explained, "Imogen's great-great-grandfather, Sam Scribblewhiskers, created the original Master Map of Friendship Forest!"

Lily and Jess knew the map well. It showed paths and streams, clearings and trees, and it had pictures of buildings, like the Toadstool Café and Spelltop School. It was divided into four sections, and a different family looked after each part. The Whizzpaws dogs had the south section, the Tappytoes deer family looked after the north, and the Bobblehop wallabies kept the east.

"My family looks after the west section of the map," Imogen explained. "It's our job to keep it safe, especially from Grizelda."

 25

Jess and Lily shared a glance. They'd already rescued the other three map sections from the witch. The scary thing was that if anything bad happened to the Master Map, the same thing happened to the forest.

When they reached Toadstool Glade, the girls gasped. Gold and silver streamers were strung between the trees, and red balloons bobbed above the tables. Painted fir cones, dotted with glitter, dangled from branches and every bush was hung with bright flowers made from tissue paper. Outside the Toadstool Café, animals

wearing

sparkly party hats

laughed and chatted.

Lily sniffed. "I smell toffee toast!"

"And coconut custard éclairs!"

said Jess.

The Longwhiskers rabbits,

who ran the café, waved. Tables

were clustered outside, laden with tiny watercress and sweet radish rolls, heart-shaped honey sandwiches, cakes, crunchy nut tarts, squidgy meringues and cookies, and jugs of fruity fizz.

"Yummy!" said Lily.

Two cats hurried over, smiling. One had silky white fur and wore a colourful necklace, while her husband was glossy black and wore a smart bow tie.

"These are my parents, Mr and Mrs Scribblewhiskers," said Imogen, and introduced the girls.

"Welcome to the party!" said Mrs

Scribblewhiskers. "Here's your special party hat, Imogen." She took a glittering crystal tiara from her big red handbag, and put it on the delighted kitten.

As Mr Scribblewhiskers tied a "Happy Birthday" sash over Imogen's shoulder, Lily noticed something sticking out of the bag.

"It's the map of the west section," she whispered to Jess.

Mr Scribblewhiskers noticed it too. "Better tuck that out of sight, dear," he said.

"Goodness, yes!" Mrs Scribblewhiskers

 29

pushed the map down into her handbag. "We always carry the map with us," she explained, "so we know it's safe."

Mr Flufftail the squirrel gathered the younger animals for a game of Nutty Scramble. Lily and Jess were nibbling toffee toast and watching the animals scamper around when they heard noises coming from the trees.

Stamp! Stamp! Crash!

The girls spun around. A tall, scowling woman stomped into the clearing. She wore a purple tunic, skinny black trousers and pointy-toed boots with spiky heels.

Her green hair twisted around her bony face like a tangle of seaweed.

"Oh no," muttered Jess. "It's Grizelda!"

"What are you doing here?" called Goldie, her hands firmly on her hips.

"I have an invitation. The silly Scribblewhiskers kitten dropped one," snapped the witch. "So I knew you'd all be here

today. The Scribblewhiskers family have something I want!"

Jess glanced at Lily. They knew what it was Grizelda wanted – the map!

The witch clapped twice. A round bottle appeared in her hands, filled with swirling green, purple, grey and blue wisps. Grizelda shook it, and four little round faces stared through the glass with large, shining eyes – the wind sprites. Goldie and the girls had already met Gale, Gust and Puff, who lived on the south, east and west winds. The wind sprites had helped Grizelda try to steal the Magical Map.

The witch uncorked the bottle and let out the purple sprite. "Huff, Huff, time to get tough!" she said.

Huff grew until he was almost as big as the girls. He hovered in the breeze, grinning. "A party!" he cried, looking around at the food and decorations. "For me? Thanks, Grizelda!"

The witch snorted. "Silly sprite! It's not for you. It's for that kitten in the soppy crown."

Huff scowled, blew a loud raspberry – *Thhhbbpp!* – and flew around, tearing at the decorations. Streamers fluttered

down and tangled around the Muddlepup puppies, who yelped in surprise.

"Ow!" cried Lola Velvetnose the mole, as a pink fir cone bounced off her head.

The Slipperslide otters wriggled to safety among clumps of moonflowers, while Lily scooped up the Nibblesqueak hamsters and popped them beneath thick tree roots.

Huff snatched a bunch of balloons and burst them on holly prickles.

Bangbangbangbangbang!

Jess grabbed Lily's hand. "We must stop him! He's ruining Imogen's birthday!"

CHAPTER THREE

Grizelda's Scary Plan

Goldie, Jess and Lily chased Huff around Toadstool Glade as he flew about, pulling down decorations. Grizelda leaned against a tree to watch them, cackling.

"Stop, Huff!" cried Lily.

But he just blew another raspberry. *Thhhbbpp!*

Suddenly Imogen gasped and pointed to one of the tables. On it was her mum's red handbag. "It's open," she whispered. "What if Huff sees the map?"

Lily whirled around. The Scribblewhiskers cats were struggling in a tangle of streamers that Huff had pulled down.

"I'll get the map," Lily said. "Don't worry, Imogen!" She edged towards the table, hoping tHuff and Grizelda wouldn't notice.

Jess held her breath.
Goldie clasped her paws
together. Lily was reaching for the
bag …

But Huff whizzed straight past her
and dived into the handbag headfirst!
He emerged and zoomed into the
air, gleefully waving the map.
"Yayyyyyy!" he shouted, and
flew to Grizelda.

"Oh no!" cried Jess.

Grizelda screeched with delight. She snatched the map from Huff, took a dropper filled with liquid from her cloak pocket and held it over the map.

Lily hurried back to join Jess, Goldie and Imogen. "What's Grizelda doing?" she asked, a jolt of worry shooting through her.

Grizelda cackled. "I'm using my Powerful Disappearance Potion, of course!"

She let one drop of greeny-brown liquid fall on to the map, then held it high so everyone could see.

The girls and the party guests watched, horrified, as the picture of the Toadstool Café started to fade. Moments later, the actual café started to fade too.

"Oh no!" Mrs Longwhiskers wailed. Little Lucy Longwhiskers burst into tears. The other animals stared in shock.

Grizelda tossed the map back to Huff. "Take that back to my tower," she ordered him. The friends watched in horror as the sprite zoomed away over the trees.

Grizelda turned back to the girls and fixed them with a nasty glare.

"That silly café disappearing is just

the start," she snarled. "A cauldron
of Powerful Disappearance Potion is
bubbling away in my tower. When I dunk
the map in it, all of the northern forest
will disappear. And then," she cackled
gleefully, "the magic will spread to the
rest of the forest. It'll *all* disappear!"

Jess stuck out her chin. "You can't do
that!"

"I can!" Grizelda screeched. "You
interfering girls and daft cat have
wrecked my plans once too often. If I
can't have the forest – then no one can!"

Horrified squeals and cries echoed

around Toadstool Glade. The party guests
crowded around Jess, Lily and Goldie,
many of them in tears. They put their
arms around each other in comfort.

Grizelda gave one last cackle, snapped
her fingers and disappeared in a cloud of

smelly yellow sparks.

"You'll help us, won't you?" pleaded
Mrs Longwhiskers, dabbing her eyes with
her apron. "You always do."

"You're our only hope," said Mr
Flufftail. His bushy tail drooped in despair.
"If you can't save us, Friendship Forest
will be gone for ever."

"We'll try our best," Lily said. She
swallowed a lump in her throat.

Jess nodded. "We won't let Grizelda
win," she promised the animals. "She's
managed to ruin Imogen's party, but we
won't let her take away your home."

Imogen's eyes were wet with tears, but she stuck out her little chin. "I'm going to help you."

Mr Scribblewhiskers put a paw on her shoulder. "I'm not sure about that," he said. "It might be dangerous."

"But I have to help!" cried Imogen. "If I hadn't dropped Lily's invitation, Grizelda wouldn't have known where to find the map. Please?"

Mr and Mrs Scribblewhiskers exchanged a look. "All right," agreed Mr Scribblewhiskers. "But stay close to your godmother."

Goldie took hold of Imogen's paw.

"We'll look after her," she promised. "And
Imogen, you mustn't blame yourself for
what happened. It's Grizelda who used
the Powerful Disappearance Potion, not
you."

They all jumped as a shadow passed
over them. The girls looked up and were

relieved to see a brightly coloured hot air balloon, with a basket hanging beneath it. A huge "Happy Birthday" banner was wrapped around the balloon. It was being towed by a stork wearing a flying helmet.

"Captain Ace!" cried Lily.

"Am I too late?" he asked. "Have I missed the party?"

Jess grinned. She'd had an idea. "The party's not happening now – thanks to that horrible Grizelda. Could you take us to her tower?"

Captain Ace gasped as he looked down at the clearing, and nearly dropped the rope in his beak. "That mean old witch!" he exclaimed. "Of course I'll take you."

He tugged on a rope. Bubbles tumbled out of the bottom of the balloon and it drifted gently towards the ground. A ladder made of plaited vines tumbled down from the basket, and the girls, Goldie and Imogen scrambled on board.

"Good luck!" called the Scribblewhiskers cats and all the other animals, as they rose into the air.

"You can do it!" cried Lucy Longwhiskers.

Lily and Jess shared a worried glance.

 46

Could they defeat Grizelda this time? If they failed, Friendship Forest would disappear for good.

CHAPTER FOUR

Grizelda's Tower

Far below the hot air balloon, trees, streams and little houses raced past. In the far distance, on the other side of a river, stood a grey, gloomy tower.

"That's Grizelda's home," said Lily, pointing it out to Imogen, who was in the crook of her arm. Imogen shuddered.

 49

"Could you land behind the tower?" Jess called to Captain Ace.

He nodded. Using the rope in his beak, he towed the balloon around Grizelda's tower, and landed them on blackened ground that was studded with wilted weeds. The friends clambered out of the basket.

"I'll wait for you here in case you need a speedy getaway," promised Captain Ace. "Good luck!"

Goldie led the way, tiptoeing around the tower to the front. Suddenly, she stopped. Huff was hovering over the

doorstep, and he was sniffing. Tears trickled down his face.

"He's upset," Goldie said.

The sprite looked up. He scowled at the four friends and blew a raspberry. *Thhhbbpp!*

"Huff!" Jess called. "What's wrong?"

Out came the sprite's tongue again.

Thhhbbpp!

"Being rude won't make things better," said Lily. "Won't you tell us what's wrong? Maybe we can help."

The sprite sniffed. "It's *my* birthday, too." He buried his face in his hands and sobbed.

Imogen's eyes were wide. "No wonder he's upset," she whispered. "I can't imagine Grizelda singing 'Happy Birthday' to him."

"Poor Huff," said Lily, softly. "Let's sing it to him instead."

"Not too loud, though," said Goldie, "in

case Grizelda hears!"

They began to sing. "Happy birthday to—"

But Huff poked out his tongue. *Thhhbbpp!*

The friends were mystified.

"Now what's wrong?" asked Lily.

The sprite scowled. "What's the point of a birthday with no presents?" He flew over to a tree stump and turned his back on them.

Imogen turned to the others, her whiskers drooping. "He's having a horrible birthday," she said. "Where can

we find him a present? There's nothing nice round Grizelda's nasty tower."

"You're being very kind to Huff, but we'll have to try and find a gift later," Jess said. "We've got to hurry up and find the map! Let's slip into the tower while he's not looking."

They carefully opened the heavy front door and crept inside. Immediately, they all clutched their noses. They were in a damp, dark hallway that smelled of mould and unwashed socks.

"What a pong!" whispered Imogen.

"We need to climb up and find

54

Grizelda's potion room," said Jess, remembering the last time she, Lily and Goldie had been there. She knew that Grizelda made her potions in the rooms at the top of the tower. They crept up a spiral stone staircase as quietly as they could. Around and around they went, higher and higher. Cobwebs brushed their hair and spiders scuttled along the banister.

At the very top of the stairs, a battered door stood slightly open. From inside came the sound of Grizelda humming a horrible tune to herself. They'd found her!

"Sludge and slime, with a perfect rhyme

And a nasty smell, make the perfect spell.

I'll be grinning ear to ear

When I make the forest disappear!"

The girls peeped inside. Grizelda was dropping handfuls of foul-smelling green slime into a big cauldron that hung over a

flickering fireplace. The potion inside the cauldron bubbled and spat, sending up sludge-coloured clouds of steam.

"How clever I am," Grizelda said, grinning widely. She picked up the map from where it rested on the table and held it over the cauldron. "So long, Friendship Forest," the witch cackled. "In it goes. One, two—"

"No!" cried Jess and Lily together, and

burst into the room.

The witch's mouth fell open. "How did you get here so quickly?" she said with a scowl.

Jess hurtled towards her. Grizelda leapt back, holding the map high in the air. Her face twisted into a furious snarl.

"How dare you set foot in my tower!" she screeched.

"Give us the map!" Lily yelled. "We

won't let you hurt the forest!"

Goldie and Imogen rushed into the room too. The four friends all ran at Grizelda, but she darted aside, her cloak swirling around her.

"You won't stop me this time," the witch sneered. "Watch!"

And she tossed the map into the cauldron.

Lily and Jess gasped. Goldie gave a cry of horror.

"No!" wailed Imogen. "Now all of the forest will disappear!"

Grizelda fished around in the cauldron

 59

and pulled out the map between her long nails. She showed it to the friends: the map was already fading. First the lines that marked paths and rivers grew faint, then the homes and shops.

Grizelda tossed her green hair, her eyes flashing with triumph. "I've won!" she cried. "At last I've got the better of you!" She danced around, her high heels clicking on the stone floor. "Say goodbye to your precious forest!"

Imogen mewed in distress. Lily scooped her up and the four friends looked at each other, too horrified to speak.

Huff had appeared, hovering in the doorway. Grizelda tossed the map to him. "Don't let the silly fools get their hands on it," she snapped. "Not that they could do anything if they did. My spell is cast!"

"Yes, Grizelda," mumbled Huff. He whizzed out of the window and flew

away on the wind.

The girls felt totally helpless. They'd failed, and now Friendship Forest was doomed.

CHAPTER FIVE

Imogen's Promise

Grizelda pulled a wand from inside her cloak. "Now I'll deal with you!" she snarled, and pointed it at the girls, Goldie and Imogen.

"You won't!" cried Jess. She ran to the bubbling cauldron and kicked it as hard as she could. It tipped over, and the potion

 63

spread over the floor, towards the witch's feet.

"Urggh!" Grizelda yelled. She leapt on to a chair. "Nooo! My feet will vanish!"

"Quick!" cried Lily.

While Grizelda was distracted, the friends raced from the room and back down the spiral staircase. On the way, Lily glimpsed the forest from a window and gasped. Already it wasn't as green as it ought to be. "The trees!

Over in the north! They're fading!"

As they left the tower, Huff zoomed around them. *Thhhbbpp!* He waved the map. "All the trees will soon disappear!" he laughed. "Everything will." Then he shot up to the top of the tower and perched there.

Jess looked at Lily, horrified. "The Friendship Tree!" she said. "If that disappears, we'll never be able to get home!"

"Oh no!" cried Goldie. "Let's ask Captain Ace to take us there now. You girls must go home while you still can."

But Lily shook her head. "We can't leave yet," she said.

Jess took Lily's hand. "We have to save the forest first. We have to get the map from Huff."

Goldie's whiskers trembled as if she was about to cry. "You're the best friends the forest could have," she said. But then she stood tall. "Come on, let's hurry!"

They dashed around the back of the tower to where Captain Ace was waiting with the hot air balloon.

"Captain, please could you take us up near Huff?" Lily asked, pointing to where the wind sprite was sitting on the roof.

Captain Ace pulled a rope and bubbles shot out from the balloon. "All aboard!" he cried.

They drifted upwards, Ace guiding the balloon so it didn't bump into the tower. When they were level with the top, they could hear Huff singing quietly.

"Happy birthday to me,

No fun, no party,

Happy birthday dear me-ee …"

"Huff!" Goldie called. "Please give us the map."

Thhhbbpp!

"Please," Lily begged. "Give it back before Friendship Forest is gone for ever. It's your home too, isn't it?"

THHHBBPP!

Imogen scrambled up so she could see Huff over the edge of the basket. "Huff," she called, "it's my birthday too. Give me the map, and I'll share my presents with you."

Huff frowned thoughtfully. The girls held their breath. Was the sprite tempted?

"I won't share," he said. "But give me your biggest birthday present, and I'll give you the map."

Imogen purred in delight. "I'll give you my biggest present! I promise!"

Lily kissed the kitten's fluffy cheek. "Well done, Imogen!" she said.

"That's so generous of you," Jess added.

Together, they all flew back to

 69

Toadstool Glade. Captain Ace beat his powerful wings, drawing the balloon through the air, while Huff whizzed along beside him, blowing raspberries to himself. As they drifted along, Lily and Jess could hardly bear to look at the northern part of the forest, where the beautiful colours were now pale. There were bare gaps where trees should be.

At Toadstool Glade, the tables were still laden with food and presents, and the animals had put the decorations Huff pulled down back in place. But there was a sad, empty place where the Toadstool

Café should have been.

Imogen and her friends jumped from the basket and ran to tell her parents about her promise. Meanwhile, Huff hovered over the presents, rubbing his hands in glee.

Huff picked up each present in turn, shaking it and sniffing it. His eyes went

wide when he spotted the largest one – a round present wrapped in flowery paper with a big red bow.

"It's mine!" he shrieked in excitement as he tore away the paper. Out bounced a huge yellow beach ball. "Wheeee!" he yelled, dropping the map. "I've never had a ball! This is the best birthday present ever!" He ran after it as it bounced across Toadstool Glade, throwing the map aside.

Imogen and her parents had hurried over, and Imogen darted to pick up the map. "Hooray!" she cried. "We've got it!"

"Thanks to you," said Goldie.

They all hugged each other in delight.
Then Lily pulled away, her face falling.
"We still haven't saved the forest," she
reminded them. "How can we get all the
places on the map to come back?"

CHAPTER SIX

Friends Together

The girls, Goldie and the Scribblewhiskers family were huddled around the map. Nearly all of the lines and pictures had disappeared – it would soon be blank. All around them, the trees and flowers were growing faint.

"What are we going to do?" wondered

Mr Scribblewhiskers, tugging at his bow tie anxiously.

Jess turned to Imogen's parents. "Imogen told us how good you are at drawing. Could you redraw the Master Map?"

Mr Scribblewhiskers shook his head sadly. "So much of the forest has disappeared that we'll have to redraw all four parts of the map," he said, "not just our northern section."

"We couldn't possibly remember everything," Mrs Scribblewhiskers added.

Goldie drew Jess and Lily aside. "The

Friendship Tree will soon be gone for ever, too," she said quietly. "Girls, I'm so sorry. But you must leave Friendship Forest while you can."

Tears welled up in the girls' eyes.

"If we leave," said Jess, her voice trembling, "we'll never be able to come back."

"I know," whispered Goldie.

Lily began to cry. "I can't bear to

leave all our friends in trouble!"

Goldie took their hands in each of their paws. "Come on," she said. "Let's slip away – we don't have time for goodbyes."

Their hearts breaking, the girls hurried away with Goldie, leaving Toadstool Glade and the Scribblewhiskers family behind them. They ran through the fading trees, past the familiar houses, and reached the Friendship Tree. To their horror, they saw that the tree was as faint as a wisp of smoke.

Goldie darted forward to touch the trunk and make the door back

to Brightley Meadow appear, just as she always did. But her paw went straight through it. She looked at the girls, her eyes swimming with tears. "We're too late. I'm so sorry!"

Lily gave a cry and turned to Jess in despair. "We can't go back home! We'll never see our families again!"

Jess shook her head, unable to believe it. "We've got to try," she said, her voice trembling. "But what can we do?"

Goldie gathered the girls into a hug. They buried their faces in her beautiful, soft fur.

Then Jess pulled back – over Goldie's shoulder, she'd spotted an amazing sight. Animals were creeping silently into the clearing. The Scribblewhiskers cats, the Flufftail squirrels, the Littlestripe badgers, the Twinkletail mice, Mr and Mrs Cleverfeather, their owl friends ... Even Captain Ace flew down with his balloon. He pulled the vine ladder from the basket, and out climbed the Paddlefoot beavers, the Woollyhop sheep and a host of frogs, hedgehogs and guinea pigs.

"Everyone's gathering at the Friendship Tree," said Goldie.

"We all want to te bogether," Mr Cleverfeather started, removing his monocle and dabbing his eyes. "I mean, be together. At the end."

The girls and their animal friends gathered into a circle. Paws held wings and hands. Lily looked around at all the familiar faces they'd met on their many adventures – adventures across the whole of the forest …

An idea struck her like sunshine breaking through the clouds. "This doesn't have to be the end!" she cried. "We can save Friendship Forest!"

Heads bobbed up. Paws dabbed tears. Faces looked at her in hope.

"How?" asked Jess with excitement.

"Mr and Mrs Scribblewhiskers," said

Lily, "you said the map's too big for you to draw."

The cats nodded.

"And you can't remember everything," Lily said.

"Yes!"

Lily flung her arms wide. "All the animals are here! If everyone tells you about their own little corner of the forest, you needn't remember anything. Just draw!"

Jess's eyes sparkled. "Brilliant!" she said, and got her own drawing pencil out of her pocket. "I'll help!"

Lily called out. "You'll all help, won't you?"

There was a great shout of "Yes!" and a chorus of excited squeaks, squeals, snorts, meows and woofs. The girls grinned at each other. Friendship Forest was going to be saved after all – by working together!

"Wait!" Mrs Scribblewhiskers's paws went to her face. "We've no pencils! We need colours! And there's no time to get them!"

CHAPTER SEVEN

Picture Perfect

"Pencils?" Captain Ace squawked. "Hold on!" He dived headfirst into his balloon basket and reappeared clutching a present. He handed it to Imogen. "Happy Birthday!"

Imogen tore off the spotty wrapping paper to reveal a big box of colouring

pencils, paints and paper. "That's perfect, Captain Ace!" she cried. "Thank you!"

Imogen handed out the pencils and paints to the animals gathered around the map. Lottie Littleleap the goat, who loved art, offered to draw the west of the forest. Mrs Scribblewhiskers did the north, and Mr Scribblewhiskers did the east. Jess worked on the south, while Imogen went from one to the other, helping to paint streams, bushes and cottages. Lily sharpened pencils and Goldie rubbed out mistakes. All the animals chipped in to tell the map-drawers what to put where – all

the houses, waterfalls, trees and bushes.

Even as they worked, the girls could
see things disappearing around them. The
candyfloss bushes around the Friendship
Tree had vanished completely and even
the grass was looking faint.

"We have to hurry!" Jess whispered to
Lily anxiously.

Very soon, all four maps were finished. Lily gathered them up and laid them on the ground together. Everyone held their breath.

Immediately, the trees and flowers became brighter, until they were as colourful as ever. The candyfloss bushes popped back into view. As the animals stamped and cheered and clapped their paws, Jess and Lily stood hand in hand, anxiously watching the Friendship Tree. One by one, its silver leaves began to gleam again, and finally its trunk was a solid, rich dark brown.

A great cheer went up. "Hooray!"

The two girls
threw their
arms around
each other.

"It's going to
be OK!" cried
Jess.

Lily nodded
joyfully. "We
can go home!"

The animals danced, pranced and
skipped. "Hooray for Lily and Jess!" they
cheered. "Hooray for Imogen and Goldie!

Hooray for Friendship Forest!"

At Toadstool Glade, everyone was getting ready to celebrate by holding Imogen's birthday party once more. The Muddlepups and Scruffypaws dogs rearranged the tables and chairs. Mr Longwhiskers organised a chain of animals to bring party food out of the Toadstool Café – which had now reappeared – passing it from paw to paw, and arranging it in a delicious spread on the tables.

"It's Huff's birthday, too," Imogen said

to the girls. "I wish he could come and share my party."

"He can't be far away," said Lily. "If we sing 'Happy Birthday' really loudly, perhaps he'll hear."

The three friends sang at the tops of their voices. In a few moments, the sprite whizzed into the clearing, still bouncing

his yellow ball.

Imogen pulled off her birthday sash. "Huff," she said, "will you share my birthday party?"

But to their surprise, Huff flung himself on to one of the chairs and burst into tears.

"Oh no!" cried Imogen. "What's wrong?"

CHAPTER EIGHT

Celebration!

Huff sniffed loudly and wiped his nose on the beach ball. "I miss my brothers," he told the girls and Imogen. "What's the point of a party if my brothers aren't here with me?"

"I know," said Jess, remembering how she'd felt at the thought of not seeing her

dad again. "Friends are great, but family's important, too."

Behind the girls, Goldie gave a warning cry. "Look out!"

Lily and Jess spun round to see an orb of dirty yellow light zooming towards them.

"Grizelda!" Lily cried.

All of the animals huddled together as the orb exploded into smelly sparks. There stood Grizelda, purple with fury.

"You girls ruined my plan AGAIN!" she screamed. She stamped her high heels and her green hair lashed about, tying itself in

knots. "You'll pay for it this time!"

A voice said, "You're the one who ruins

things, Grizelda."

Lily and Jess stared at each other in

surprise. It was Huff!

The wind sprite floated over

to the witch. "Stop spoiling

everything," he told her,

"and have some fun!"

"Fun?" Grizelda

screeched. "FUN?"

She was so angry

that her hands

were balled into fists

and she was shaking.

Huff picked up the beach ball from where it had rolled to a stop. "Catch!" he said, and he tossed it at Grizelda.

The ball hit Grizelda in the middle of her stomach. "Oof!" she grunted – and something fell from inside her cloak, smashing to the ground. It was the sprite bottle.

Lily and Jess gasped. Three tiny sprites – Gale, Gust and Puff – sat wide-eyed amid broken glass. Then they grew until they were as big as Huff and whirled through the air.

"We're free!" cried Gale.

"Hooray!" yelled Puff.

Gust gave a joyful burp.

"We're back together!"
cried Huff. He zoomed to meet
them, and the brothers whizzed
around each other.

Jess laughed. "They're like a
happy whirlwind!"

The sight of the
playing sprites seemed
to make Grizelda
even angrier.

"Just wait!" she screeched. "I'll have my revenge! You lot haven't heard the last of Grizelda!" With a snap of her fingers, she vanished in a spatter of stinking sparks.

The animals broke into cheers and the party began properly at last. Everyone feasted until they were full. Melody Sweetsong the nightingale sang and Grace Woollyhop the lamb played her flute, so all the animals could dance. The wind sprites played with the beach ball, but not by throwing it – by blowing it!

"I'm sharing it with my brothers," Huff explained to the girls and Goldie. "But

you can have it back afterwards, Imogen."

"It's yours," she told him, putting a paw on his shoulder.

"We're sorry we helped Grizelda," said Gale.

"She trapped us," said Puff. "If we didn't obey, we'd have been kept in her bottle for ever."

Gust just burped.

Goldie smiled. "You're all forgiven." She and the girls laughed as the sprites looped the loop together, making a colourful blur.

Eventually, Jess dropped a kiss on

Imogen's fluffy head. "What a lovely party! But now it's time for us to go home."

The girls were sad to leave, but this time, they were also glad that they could go home.

Imogen hurled herself at the girls. "Thank you for my brilliant adventure!

This birthday's been the best ever. Come and visit soon, won't you?"

"Of course we will," said Lily. "And if ever Friendship Forest is in danger, we'll be back to help save it."

"We know you will," Goldie said.

After the girls had said their goodbyes, and eaten one last slice of hazelnut and rose petal cake, Goldie took them back to the Friendship Tree. She touched the trunk and this time the familiar door opened.

Goldie held the girls' hands, her green eyes shining. "Goodbye," she said, and kissed their cheeks. They threw their

arms around

her, hugging her

tightly.

Then Lily

and Jess stepped

through the door,

into golden light,

and the next

moment they

were back in Brightley Meadow. They

ran through the field, over the stepping

stones and back to Helping Paw. There

they found the fox cubs still tugging at

the red chewy bone. It had almost split in

the middle!

Jess laughed. "They're no good at sharing, are they? Not like Imogen."

"I'll fix that," said Lily. She took the bone and snapped it into two pieces. "There you are," she told the foxes. "You can have half each."

The fox cubs settled down together, chewing happily, and Lily and Jess sat beside them. All around, animals were playing in their pens, enjoying the soft sunshine. Flowers danced in the breeze, and from indoors came the sounds of Lily's parents, chatting away as they cared

for their patients.

Lily turned to Jess. "It's scary to think we might never have been able to come back, isn't it?"

Jess nodded. "Friendship Forest is the most magical, beautiful place." She grinned at Lily. "But home is pretty wonderful, too."

The End

Join best friends Lily and Jess for a very special adventure with Bertie Bigroar the lion cub. Little Bertie has a big heart, but can be shy sometimes.

Can the girls help Bertie be brave like his brothers, and defeat the wicked witch Grizelda?

Find out in the next Magic Animal Friends book,

Bertie Bigroar Finds His Voice

Turn over for a sneak peek ...

Lily Hart and her best friend, Jess Forester, were kneeling on the sunny lawn in Lily's garden.

"Here, girl!" called Lily.

"Here, boy!" said Jess.

They each held out a bone-shaped biscuit. But the two Chow Chow puppies were so busy wrestling with each other that they didn't pay any attention. Their golden fur fluffed up all around them like cotton wool, and their tiny pink tongues stuck out as they panted.

They had been found wandering the woods with hurt paws that morning.

Someone had brought them in to the Helping Paw Wildlife Hospital, which Lily's parents ran from a barn in the bottom of their garden. Now the puppies were better, and in just a few hours, their owner would be arriving to pick them up.

Lily held up the biscuits again. "Here, doggies!"

"Maybe if we hide, they'll come and look for us," said Jess.

The girls crept over to a bush and ducked down behind it. Then they both called together: "Here, puppies!"

Sure enough, the puppies stopped

barking. Then the girls heard trotting paws, and the two Chow Chows dashed around the side of the bush.

"Good dogs!" said Lily, laughing as she gave them each a biscuit.

"Let's try it again," said Jess. "Only this time, we'll hide behind a pen."

The girls backed away, then hid behind a rabbit hutch. "Here, puppies!" they called together.

Paws came padding towards them. Then a furry golden face peeked round the side of the hutch...

Jess gasped. "Goldie!"

The golden cat purred as she wound her way between their legs, tail upright in greeting. Jess and Lily bent to stroke their friend. Goldie was no ordinary cat – she came from the magical world of Friendship Forest, where the animals could talk and walked on their hind legs.

"You know what this means," said

Read

Bertie Bigroar Finds His Voice

to find out what happens next!

Magic
Animal Friends

Can Jess and Lily save the magic of Friendship Forest from Grizelda? Read all of series eight to find out!

COMING SOON!
Look out for
Jess and Lily's
next adventure:
Bertie Bigroar Finds His Voice!

3 stories in 1!

www.magicanimalfriends.com

If you like
Magic Animal Friends,
you'll love…

Welcome to Animal Ark!

Animal-mad Amelia is sad
about moving house, until she discovers
Animal Ark, where vets look after all
kinds of animals in need.

*Join Amelia and her friend Sam for a
brand-new series of animal adventures!*

Magic
Animal Friends
Can you keep the secret?

There's lots of fun for everyone at
www.magicanimalfriends.com

Play games and explore the secret world of
Friendship Forest, where animals can talk!

Join the
Magic Animal Friends Club!

Special competitions

Exclusive content

All the latest Magic Animal Friends news!

To join the Club, simply go to

www.magicanimalfriends.com/join-our-club/